NIKI DALY has won numerous awards at home and abroad for his lyrical writing and lively illustrations. *Not So Fast, Songololo*, winner of The Katrine Harries Award and a US Parents' Choice Award, paved the way for post-apartheid South African children's books. Among his many Frances Lincoln books are the bestselling *Jamela* series. "bursting with life and charm" – TES, *Once Upon a Time*, an Honor Winner in the US Children's Africana Book Award, *Ruby Sings the Blues*, *Pretty Salma* and *No More Kisses for Bernard*. In 2009 Niki Daly was awarded the Molteno Gold Medal for his major contribution towards South African children's literature. He lives with his wife, the illustrator Jude Daly, in Kleinmond, South Africa.

For the Mdingi family

JANETTA OTTER-BARRY BOOKS

Text and illustrations copyright © Niki Daly 2012

The right of Niki Daly to be identified as the author and illustrator of this
work has been asserted by him in accordance with the Copyright,
Designs and Patents Act, 1988 (United Kingdom).

First published in Great Britain in 2012 by
Frances Lincoln Children's Books,
74-77 White Lion Street,
London N1 9PF

www.franceslincoln.com

First paperback published in Great Britain in 2014

A catalogue record for this book is available from the British Library

ISBN 978-1-84780-494-5

Printed in China

1 3 5 7 9 8 6 4 2

The

Herd Boy

NIKI DALY

F

FRANCES LINCOLN
CHILDREN'S BOOKS

"Wake up, Malusi!" Mama calls.

Inside, the hut is still dark.

Outside, the air is cool and the sun is rising – first a red rim along the surrounding hills, then turning to gold as it rises and starts warming the village.

Mielie pap is steaming in the pot.

"Eat up!" says Mama. "A boy cannot work on an empty stomach."

Malusi looks after his grandfather's sheep and goats.

It's a big job for a small boy.

"Pweew! Pweew!" Malusi's shrill whistling drives the sheep out of Grandfather's *kraal*.

By the time they reach the grazing slopes, the earth is hot beneath his bare feet.

Malusi shields his eyes against the sun's glare and looks up. There, high in the sky, flying in wide circles, he spots a Black Eagle.

He places his feet carefully as he moves through the bush where puffadders doze, coiled up and unseen.

He keeps the sheep and goats from straying towards the deep *donga*, which is easy to fall into, but hard to climb out of.

You have to be awake, and you have to be brave to be a herd boy.

Along the *krans*, a troop of baboons gather. If they come down, he will use his voice and a handful of stones to drive them back.

"Woof!" He hears Koko barking.

That means his friend, Lungisa, is only a shout away.

Lungisa is older than Malusi and has his own dog.

Sometimes they meet and play games while the sheep graze. Lungisa always wants to play two-man-football and stick-fight. Malusi likes a challenge. Koko jumps out of their way as they kick up the dust.

"*Shu!*" yells Malusi, in the middle of the fight. "I'm hot!" So they take a break while he removes his blanket . . . slowly . . . giving him time to plan how to win a few points. But he never does.

Lungisa is the champion footballer *and* champion stick-fighter. Still, Malusi is a quick learner. He knows he must keep his eye on the ball and move out of harm's way during a stick-fight.

It's lunchtime and Zolika, his older sister, brings their lunch.

Every day it is the same thing – *umvubo*, a sour mixture of curdled milk and mielie pap. He and Lungisa always eat it all up and scrape the tin bowls with their fingers.

"When I grow up," says Lungisa, "I'm going to play football for Bafana-Bafana."

"When I grow up," says Malusi quietly, "I'm going to be President."

Lungisa laughs so loudly that it sets the baboons off.

"Waahoo! Waahoo!" they holler back.

Zolika collects the bowls. "Malusi is clever," she says. "He can be anything he likes."

Malusi is glad when Lungisa disappears into the dip to join his flock.

Malusi likes being on his own – just him and his shadow. Dead quiet and as still as a mountain, he watches the ground, where two columns of termites are on the march. *Eish!* Such hard workers – all working together.

If he sees one on its own, he feels sorry for it, and says, *"Hamba!* Go away, little gogga – go and join your people."

Push-push, roll-roll,
push-push, roll-roll,
Malusi smiles at the dung beetle who never gives up. It rests in Malusi's shadow and then pushes on into the harsh sunlight.

It reminds Malusi what he must still do – collect some fresh dung to give to the shopkeeper, uMdinga, who will add it to the soil in his garden. In return, Malusi's mother will receive some fresh vegetables.

He practises his counting as he scoops up the dung pebbles: *nye* – one . . . *mbini* – two . . . *ntathu* – three . . . until the sack is filled.

Push-push, roll-roll,
push-push, roll-roll,
Malusi smiles at the dung beetle
who never gives up. It rests in Malusi's
shadow and then pushes on into the
harsh sunlight.

It reminds Malusi what he must still
do – collect some fresh dung to give to
the shopkeeper, uMdinga, who will add
it to the soil in his garden. In return,
Malusi's mother will receive some fresh
vegetables.

He practises his counting as he scoops
up the dung pebbles: *nye* – one . . .
mbini – two . . . *ntathu* – three . . . until
the sack is filled.

Haai wena! When he looks up, there's
an old baboon sitting on a rock – and it is
much too close to the baby lambs
and kids.

Malusi shakes his stick and shouts,
"Hamba!"

The baboon is thin and looks hungry.
When he opens his jaws, he is missing
one fang. Still, Malusi does not like the
look of him, and when he suddenly climbs
off the rock and moves forward, it is time
to shout much louder.

"Lungisaaaaa! Kokooooo!"

His voice echoes off the krans.

Now the bush is filled with Malusi's cries and the bleating of the frightened herd.

The baboon is among the sheep and goats! If he does not take a young one, he will scare the animals towards the donga. Malusi moves cautiously among the flock – stick at the ready.

Then he spots the baboon's tail, hears the cry of a lamb and sees the dust of a struggle.

"Maluuuusi!"

It's Lungisa coming with Koko.

Koko smells the baboon and dashes in between the frightened animals – who clear a ring for the fight. Lungisa and Malusi push themselves forwards, ready to help Koko.

But there is no fight.

Koko's blood-curdling growls and bared teeth have changed the baboon's mind. He lets go of the bleeding lamb and scuttles back up the slope.

The lamb is injured, but still alive. Maybe Grandfather can put some medicine on its wounds and make it better.

For now, Malusi wraps his blanket around the little lamb and pats Koko.

"I wish I had a dog like you," he says to the panting dog.

"He's like Baby Jake," brags Lungisa.

Malusi has to agree. Koko is short but very powerful, like the famous boxer – Baby Jake Matlala.

The heat has gone out of the day, and it is time to go home. Lungiso offers to carry uMdingi's dung so that Malusi can carry the injured lamb. Koko barks at the herd, driving them down the slope towards the dirt road that leads to the kraal.

> *"Yes, Mother, we are hungry!*
> *Is the fire burning?*
> *Is the food cooking?*
> *Yes, Mother, we are returning!"*

Malusi and Lungisa sing this song along the dirt road. Then they stop.

"Look," says Lungisa. "A car is coming!"

Malusi sees it approach in a cloud of dust.

They move the sheep to the side of the road. But the car does not pass. Instead, it slows down and stops.

"Who has such a smart, shiny car?" wonders Malusi.

Slowly, the back window opens and an old man with a face as lined as the krans smiles at them.

"*Molweni!*" greets the old man.

"*Molo Tat'omkhulu*." The boys return his greeting.

He tells them that, when he was a young boy, he also wore a red blanket and looked after sheep. Malusi looks at the beautiful shirt he is wearing now and quickly looks down.

"So what do you boys want to be when you grow up?" asks the old man.

"To play for Bafana-Bafana," answers Lungisa.

Malusi is too shy to answer, so Lungisa answers for him.

"He wants to be the President," says Lungisa, giggling.

Then the old man sees what Malusi has been carrying and says, "Ah, a boy who looks after his herd will make a very fine leader. *Sala kahle*, Mr President."

The sun has dipped behind the hills, casting long shadows across the veldt.

The soft padding of hooves on clay makes gentle music. Voices can be heard coming from the kraal.

Malusi hopes his grandfather will not be angry because he has brought home a wounded lamb. Surely he will know that Malusi has done his very best to save it.

Maybe the little lamb will survive.

Before bedtime, a pup is brought to Malusi.

"uMdingi sent this for you," says his grandfather. "I'm told that Koko is his dad, so those baboons had better watch out!"

Malusi smiles and opens his blanket for the pup to crawl under.

All is well.

In the darkness of the hut, Malusi repeats the words of the old man:

"A boy who looks after his herd will make a fine leader."

Then he closes his tired eyes and falls asleep. . .

where a dream
is waiting to be dreamed.

A Note from the Author

Many great men come from humble beginnings. One such was the boy, David, of the Old Testament, who looked after his father's flocks and later rose to become a king. Muhammad, too, spent part of his boyhood, in all weathers and amid dangers, tending to his family's herd.

A great and much-loved man of our own time – former President Nelson Rolihlahla Mandela, also came from a humble, rural background. Just who could have predicted that a herd boy from the village of Qunu in the Transkei would, one day, become a great world leader?

Though our childhoods may appear accidental – some luckier than others – they so often seem custom-made for the adults we become. So I ask, 'What is there in the life of a herd boy that would help prepare him to become the shepherd of a nation?'

Glossary:

Mielie pap (Afrikaans) *mee-lee-pup*, maize porridge

Kraal (Dutch/S African) *kraa-el*, an enclosure for animals near a homestead.

Krans (from German: *Kranz*) *kraa-ns*, an overhanging cliff-face

Shu! (Xhosa shu-shu) *shoo*, hot.

Umvubo (Xhosa) *oom-voo-boo*, a mixture of curdled sour milk and maize porridge

Bafana (Xhosa) *bar-far-nah*, boys, (Bafana-Bafana is a South African football team)

Eish! (Xhosa; slang) *eesh*, exclamation expressing surprise

Humba! (Xhosa) *hum-bah*, go or go away

Gogga (Afrikaans) *chaw-chaw* ('*ch*' as in '*loch*'), a little insect

Nye, mbini, ntathu (Xhosa) '*n-yeh*, '*m-bee-nee*, '*n-taa-too*, numbers one, two and three

uMdingi (Xhosa) *oo-m-dingy*, u is the title Mr, hence Mr Mdingi.

Haai wena! (Xhosa) *high-where-nah*, exclamation of alarm as in 'oh no!' or 'gosh!'

Molweni (Xhosa) *mawl-where-nee*, hello (plural)

Molo Tat'omkhulu (Xhosa) *Maw-lor taa-toom-cool-loo*, hello, Grandfather

Sala kahle! (Xhosa) *Sah-lah kah-shlay*, stay well!

Veld(t) (Afrikaans) *felt*, S African rural landscape most often used for grazing or farming

COLLECT ALL THE JAMELA BOOKS BY NIKI DALY

*"The Jamela stories of everyday life depict experiences that will
resonate with young children, irrespective of cultural background."*
The Ultimate Book Guide

Jamela's Dress was chosen by Julia Eccleshare as one of the
1001 Children's Books You Must Read Before You Grow Up

978-0-71121-449-1

978-0-71121-705-8

978-1-84507-106-6

978-1-84507-422-7

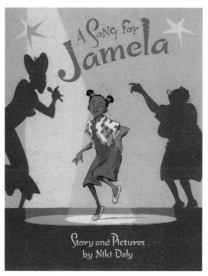

978-1-84507-871-3

Frances Lincoln titles are available from all good bookshops.
You can also buy books and find out more about your favourite titles,
authors and illustrators on our website: www.franceslincoln.com